Feb 27th 2012.

"The Plumber"

Thanks, and best wishes.

Reg & Janet Smith.

XX.

THE MAN ENGLAND FORGOT

The diary, words and poetry of Clifford Nichols illustrate his endurance, life and thinking as a serviceman and POW captured at Tobruk in the North Africa Campaign in World War II. To read his poems one can empathise with him in his situations of heartache, suffering, gratitude, sometimes humour, comradeship and hope.

This book is a dedication to him and all prisoners of war.

The Man England Forgot

Diary, Words and Poetry

A Tribute to Driver ***Clifford Nichols***, RASC

Prisoner of War 1942-45

ARTHUR H. STOCKWELL LTD.
Elms Court Ilfracombe Devon
Established 1898

First published in Great Britain, 1998

British Library Cataloguing-in-Publication Data.
A catalogue record for this book is available from the British Library.

ISBN 0 7223 3191-6
Printed in Great Britain by
Arthur H. Stockwell Ltd.
Elms Court Ilfracombe
Devon

CONTENTS

Cover:
An illustration of places with dates visited as a soldier, then subsequently as a POW.

ACKNOWLEDGEMENTS

Appreciation from the family of Driver Nichols for the poems discovered, which will be cherished.

With thanks to his fellow POW, Frank Slater, for his sketches drawn whilst in captivity. (Note: the cover sketch has been slightly amended).

Thanks and gratitude to The British Red Cross Society, and to the Order of St John.

INTRODUCTION

Driver Nichols served in a part of the North Africa Campaign in World War Two. The title of the book, and the personal diary of prose and verse from which it is taken, represent a belated tribute to a prisoner of war.

The contents of these memoirs were only discovered after the writer's recent death and, although written by a man with no academic background, they reflect the deep patriotism, pain and courage not only of him, but of hundreds of thousands of POWs all over the world.

Driver Nichols served in the transport division of the RASC, and as such played a vital role in maintaining supplies to the troops fighting in the desert campaign.

This personal record has been put together for fellow comrades, for their families during that era and now, over fifty years later, for their younger generations.

The courage shown by these men should not be forgotten.

On behalf of **T/200033 Driver Nichols, C.,**
68 Heavy AA Regiment RA,
Royal Army Service Corps.

KEY:
OCT '41 – MID. 1943
EGYPT AND LIBYA

1. SEWA
2. FUKA
3. MADDALENA
4. CAPUZZO
5. BIR-EL-HAMMED
6. GAMBUT
7. EL-ADEM
8. SIDI-REZEGH
9. GAZALA
10. TIMINI
11. CIRENE
12. TOCRA
13. BARCE
14. MECHILI
15. MSUS
16. AGEDABIA

ITALY

17. TARANTO
18. BRINDISI
19. BARI
20. LORETO
21. GROTTAMMARE
22. ANCONA
23. RIMINI
24. FAENZA
25. BOLOGNA
26. MODENA

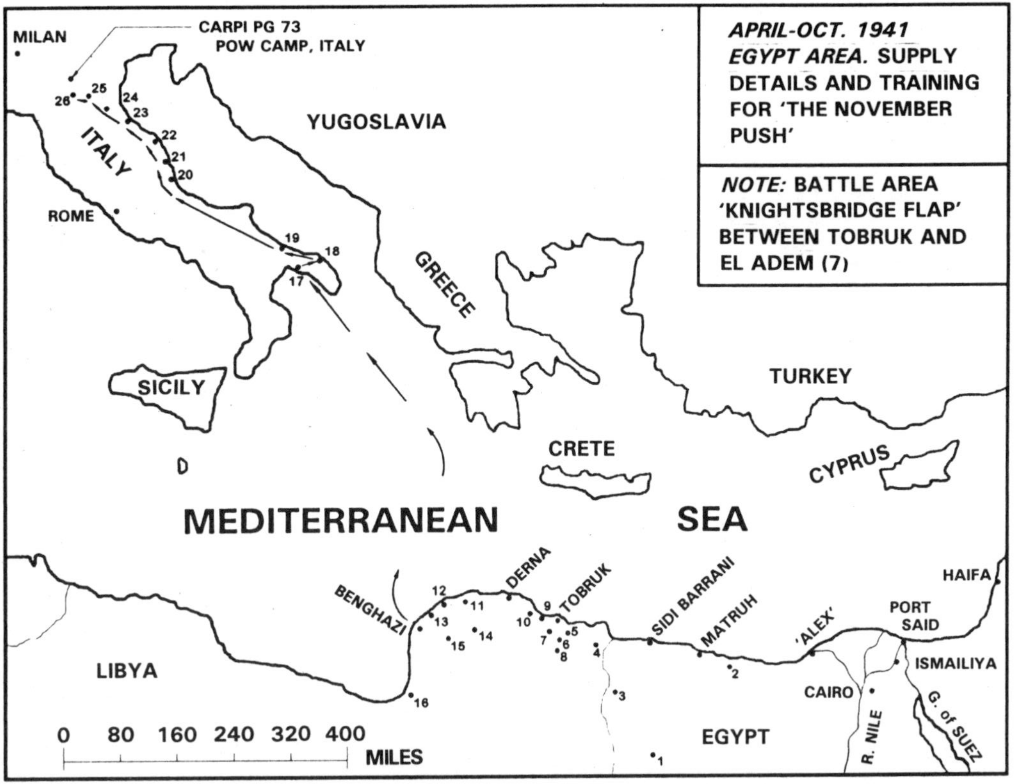

DRIVER NICHOLS' SERVICE AND CAPTURED ROUTES IN THE MIDDLE EAST

6th FEBRUARY, 1941

Embarkation, Liverpool:

The journey to Egypt was made around The Cape — this being the safest route, as opposed to the more dangerous Mediterranean route.

This 'Cape route' took Driver Nichols and his comrades via:

Bangor Bay

Freetown — Sierra Leone, Cape Town — Africa, then five wonderful days' leave ashore at **Durban**, "a place one cannot forget".

Then onwards to **Mombassa**; **Aden**; **Port Suez**; and finally, on 24th April, 1941, disembarked at **Port Tewfik, Egypt**.

Travelled by train to **Cassasine** and camped for six weeks at **TAHAG** camp.

Tel-El-Kibir, **Ismailiya** and **Mosaker** were within supply detail range, and the Egyptian Desert.

June, 1941: left TAHAG Camp and headed for **Cairo**, making camp along the way at **Kilo 4, Suez Road**. Supply details:

- **Abbassia**: British Garrison.
- **Mena**: the Pyramids of Giza are to be seen here.
- **Alexandria**: A very lovely place. Spent quite a lot of time here. Must tell you about some of the nights out here. Of 'Alex' and Cairo, I prefer Cairo.
- **Haifa** (Palestine): Went only once (on convoy), but should have loved a stay in Palestine.

[Being] stationed at Cairo was a grand holiday for us, but we were now to leave and join our AA Regiment ready for the 'November Push'.

5th October, 1941: TAHAG: Spent about fourteen days here attending lectures about what to do, and not to do on convoy work in action.

Our 'section' was 104 strong, including Lieutenant Critcher and Captain Elphinstone (OC), who was said to have done good work in Abbasinia. We had all taken a liking to our CO. Parted company with Stan, Bill and Bob.

End of *October, 1941:* left TAHAG for the "Blue". Our destination, we were told, was Tobruk.

OCTOBER, 1941

Towards Tobruk: The "November Push"

Amireyea: Our first stop was at 'Sydney Camp', about twenty miles from 'Alex'. Spent four to five days here.

El-Daba: This was a most enjoyable run for about ninety miles along the coast road of the lovely blue Mediterranean Sea.

Abu Haggag: Made camp here for four to five weeks, working from railhead to:

- **Sewa, Fuka, Sidi-Haniesh, Sidi-Ab-Salaam, Bir-El-Khamsa, El-Tarig.**
- **Fort Maddalena.**

24th November, 1941: "First flap of Push":

- **Trigh Capuzzo, Bir-El-Hammed, Gambut,** then:
- **Tobruk — Libya**
- **El Adem, Sidi Rezegh, Acroma Gazala, Timimi.**

Christmas 1941 at **Mechili**: A Christmas one won't forget. Spent Christmas Day and Boxing Day at Mechili. Our meals consisted of one tin of bully, one packet of biscuits, between two and a half pints of salt-water tea.

Msus, Agedabia: We were now travelling by road from Tobruk.

Derna: Billeted here about five weeks, supplying AA units: **Cirene, Barce, Tocra, Benghazi**. Did a few 'details' to **Mersa Matruh, Sidi Barrani**, and **Fort Capuzzo**.

Then we were sent to Benghazi to stand by ready to evacuate coastal batteries and AA units. Left Benghazi at midnight one Sunday and retreated right back to Tobruk — this was 'a drive to remember'.

Tobruk: Back at Tobruk we started working as a transport unit from the docks. In this work we had a very busy time with 'Jerry'. The unit had three months of this work and then was put in charge of a supply dump, to supply the 4th AA Brigade, and meant two trucks being kept off 'dock work'. I was very lucky in having my truck detailed as the bread and meat wagon, and really enjoyed this work.

27th May, 1942: "Knightsbridge Flap", which ended in the fall of Tobruk. Then we were sent back to base (Tobruk), but 'Jerry' decided otherwise.

21st JUNE, 1942

Taken Prisoner of War

I was taken prisoner by Jerry on the beaches at Tobruk, and handed over to the Italians on 23rd June, 1942, and at whose hands we received bad treatment until reaching a permanent camp at **Carpi**, near **Milan**, Italy.

The journey:

–	**Tobruk**	21st to 23rd June
–	**Timimi**	24th to 26th June
–	**Derna**	26th June to 2nd July
–	**Benghazi**	2nd to 22nd July

22nd July, 1942: Boarded ship *'Rovello'* and, setting sail, passed **Crete**, **Greece** and **Sicily**.

Note: RASC Records' Office, Hastings notified his wife on 22nd July, 1942 that Driver Nichols was posted "Missing 20.6.42 in the Middle East".

–	**Taranto (Italy)**	– disembarked –	26th July
–	**Brindisi**	– (transit camp) –	27th July to 1st August
–	**Attamura**	– (PG 51) –	2nd August

. . . and then moved on, passing:

- **Bari, Grottammare, Loreto, Ancona, Rimini, Faenza, Bologna, Modena**

. . . to **Carpi** (PG 73), near **Milan**, 1st September, 1942.

Note: the abbreviation PG, where it appears in this text, refers to a POW camp identification code.

The time spent at Timini, Derna, Benghazi and Attamura at the hands of the Italians will never be forgotten by those who went through it, and will make one always want to hate the Italians forever.

29th September, 1942: Visited by The Red Cross for the first time since being a POW.

Memos from Carpi:

10.11.42	Italian clothing issued to us (wearing KD until now).
23.11.42	Moved out of tents into huts.
26.11.42	A ten-word Christmas greeting card sent home through The Vatican: *"My thoughts are with you all this festive season, Clifford".*
04.12.42	Italian issue of cigarettes and tobacco cancelled, supposed shortage.
06.12.42	Italian cigarettes cut down to twenty-five per man per week and resumed on 12.12.42 to four per day.

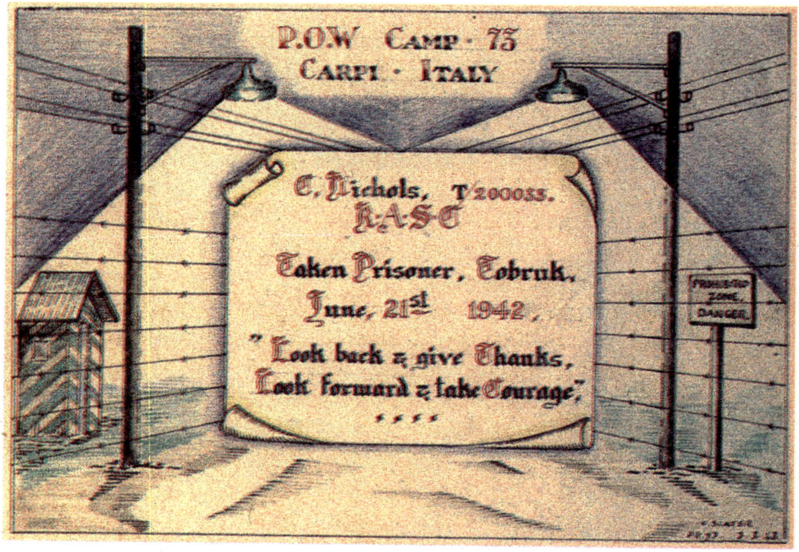

POW sketch by fellow prisoner Frank Slater.

Christmas in a POW camp, 1942 — PG 73 — Carpi, Italy

Christmas Eve. This was the day we had all been looking forward to. One parcel each for Xmas. You can well imagine our feelings at having one parcel each, after having one between four, every four days all this time. Four of us: Alf, Jack, Bill and myself received three English Christmas parcels and one Canadian. Just what we'd hoped for.

Christmas Eve was spent preparing for Christmas morn.

Christmas Morning. We were up at 7.30 a.m., as excited and happy as little children. I must say that my thoughts flew at once to my little girl and my wife at home.

At eight o'clock we had one pint of cocoa, Canadian biscuits, butter, cheese and chocolate. The rest of the morning was spent getting ready for *tiffin*.

At twelve o'clock, for Christmas dinner we had fried bread, sardines, fried onion, bully-meat-roll, steak and mac, two loaves of bread, butter, jam, cheese, pumpkin pie with cream, Christmas pudding with custard, Christmas cake and tea.

Five o'clock, Tea: bread, butter, jam, cake, cream and chocolate.

The evening spent playing cards and a 'singsong', and had two small bottles of beer (Italian pilsner). Finally, for supper; coffee, cake, chocolate and biscuits.

Quite an enjoyable day - far better than I'd had Christmas 1941, but for all that one's thoughts are constantly at home.

Christmas Day 1942, one to remember as a POW.

Boxing Day was another decent day.

New Year's Eve: Once again, thoughts of home. "Silence" was put back to 12.30 — God knows what for — we had nothing to celebrate with, and were in bed by nine o'clock.

New Year's Day 1943: Snow, frosty and very cold. Again thoughts of home with wife and family. I hope and pray I haven't to spend another whole year away from them.

We had a parcel between four on the last day of the old year and had saved a bit of 'scran' from our Christmas parcels, so as to have a decent day today.

Eight o'clock: Coffee — lousy; porridge — good.

11.30, tiffin: ½lb. steak and tomato pud each. Curried veal, tomatoes, two loaves of bread, butter, jam, cheese, apples, oranges. Fig pudding and custard.

Five o'clock, 'Skilly', Ovaltine, bread, butter, jam, cheese, cake, cream.

A good start to the New Year, but what now? The past six months as a POW have been very hard, the first five months being tortured with hunger. Things are a bit better now The Red Cross have got working, but there's a saying and, by God, it's true:

"THERE'S NO PLACE LIKE HOME".

After the New Year's celebrations, and up to mid-1943 at Carpi, there is little record of communication from Driver Nichols, except, that is, for the discovery of twenty-five beautifully hand-written poems in his Italian issued note pad. One example of these is the poem "Little Wooden Crosses".

Little Wooden Crosses.

Little Wooden Crosses
Bearing name and number.
In the hot dry desert sand
There our Comrades slumber.

Lads with whom we laughed and joked
Played games and had our fun.
Lads we slept with neath the stars
When the day was done.

Lads we fought beside through hell
Of our race the leaven,
They through tribulation come
Quickly into Heaven.

Now beneath the alien Earth.
Their tired bones rest
The only Epitaph they ask
I tried and gave my best.

But we who live on after them
A great gift, too must give
And Dedicate our lives to prove
The right to think and live

Clifford Nichols, 6th February 1912 to 3rd November 1997
For this, and for the complete book of poems, see poem section.

Also discovered from this period is the following postcard, which was sent home to his wife and four-year-old daughter. The photograph was most certainly taken before his capture.

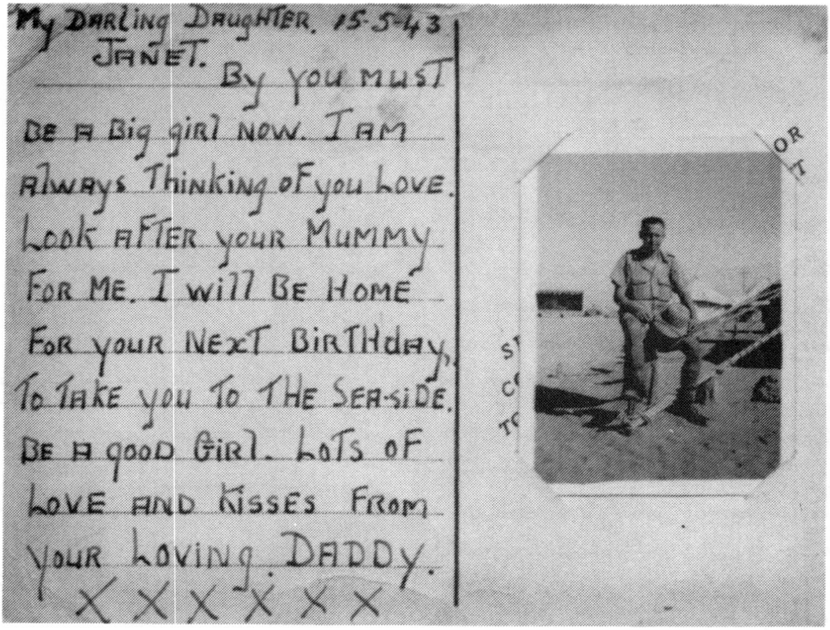

My Darling Daughter. 15-5-43
Janet.
By you must
be a big girl now. I am
always Thinking of you love.
Look after your Mummy
for me. I will be home
for your next Birthday,
To Take you To The Sea-side.
Be a good Girl. Lots of
love and kisses from
your loving Daddy.
X X X X X X

MID-1943 (ESTIMATED)

On the march to a German POW camp

Very little is know about the events of the POW's journey from Carpi, near Milan, through Austria and into Germany, except that it was horrendous. This march over the mountains must have taken some five or six months. Men unable to march were packed into cattle trucks and many comrades, already weakened from POW life died on the journey. Women from the towns and villages on route in Italy spat at the POWs as they passed, and life was generally at a very low ebb.

In Austria, life-saving potato soup was provided by The Red Cross.

Note: RASC Records' Office, Hastings notified his wife on 24th January, 1944, that Driver Nichols had been transferred from Italy to Stalag IVG in Germany, POW No. 247332.

However, Driver Nichols' dog tags were stamped Stalag IVB, which is believed to have been at Mühlberg on Elbe.

Further diary memos:

16.2.44	Bill left.
08.9.44	Left **Klingu** (35/361) for **Kleinsteinberg** (34/359).
21.9.44	Alf Left.
14.4.45	Left **Kleinsteinberg** 'on the march' away from the Yanks.
22.4.45	Left **Borna** (Elbe), this time away from the Russians.
24.4.45	Arrived near **Trebsem** *(Stalag II)*, which was in possession of the Yanks.

LIBERATED 25th APRIL, 1945, HANDED OVER TO THE 'YANKS':
"A DAY TO REMEMBER"

Note: The camps in Germany were in the Leipzig area.

POEMS OF CLIFFORD NICHOLS

Mother

There's an old-fashioned lady
Who's waiting back home
With a prayer in her heart for me,
Hoping and praying for my return
And that never again will I roam.

There's an old-fashioned cottage
In which she now sits
With a smile on her face for all,
Knowing that some day her loved one will
Return to answer her call.

There's an old-fashioned picture
That hangs on the wall
A picture that looks like me,
She looks at it daily with tears in her eyes,
While she whispers please come back to me.

There's an old-fashioned armchair
That stands on the porch,
She had it placed there just for me.
I'll cherish it dearly as I sit and dream,
When together again we will be.

There's an old-fashioned prayer
Which I often repeat,
A prayer which will always remain
God Bless Mother, and how I hope
That my prayers are not in vain.

Heart to Heart

I find it hard to say what's in
My heart Dear, when I write
It looks so "sentimental", when
It's there, in Black and White.

Memories come crowding
Back out of the happy years,
Memories of many things
Half gladness and half tears.

I falter when I would express
My hopes, and thoughts and dreams,
But, sometimes when I'm all alone
You come to me it seems
And stand beside me of old
No longer far apart. "But"
Hand in hand, "Together"
Walking and Talking
Heart to Heart.

To Our Pals in the MEF*

Here's to our Pals, though they be dead
Killed in Action by enemy lead,
Buried in Libya, under trackless sand
Far away from their beloved land.

Leaving behind, the ones they loved dear,
To answer the call, without fear,
So, here's to our Pals, may God let them lie,
For bravely they fought, and bravely they died.

* *NOTE: MEF stands for Middle East Forces.*

Our England

'Tis only an island
Rugged and small
With peace-loving people
No quarrels at all.
There's green fields and country
Cities and towns
With lots of contentment
Never no frowns.
It's the heart of an Empire
Mighty and great
Where the grandest of families
Rule in state.
Great is her history, and
Firm is her stand
For there is no place like
This little land.

A POW's Good Night

Now the day is over, night is drawing nigh
Us poor POWs on timber beds do lie,
No clean sheets, pillows, or eiderdowns so nice
Just a couple of blankets, and ten thousand lice.

But we're not downhearted, our spirits up we keep,
Through the long and weary hours
We try and get some sleep,
When the daylight cometh we're on the side of right
We'll beat these blinking Eyeties yet,
Good Night — Good Night.

Thanks

Thanks to that organisation
The Society of British Red Cross
For parcels that have been the Salvation
Of many a lad thought lost.

Cheers to a great population
For anything they may subscribe
To let this organisation
Hold up its head with pride.

Thanks to the friends of New Zealand,
Of Canada and Colonies as well
And all of those in every land
That help them do so well.

Ever Yearning

For you dear one I'm ever yearning,
How could I ever forget
My thoughts like homing birds returning
Where the heart is set.

Lead me down the path of peace
To memory's golden door
Away from all this 'sin and din'
And tragedy of war.

We have our love, life cannot cheat us,
Of this splendid thing
No power disheartens or defeats us,
Time will only bring

New buds of hope fresh flowers of faith,
To bloom in love's green bowers,
When God at last restores to us
Those lost and wasted hours.

To My Mother and Father

Some day when the war is over
I'll come back again to thee,
When peace once more shall bless this earth
I'll safely cross the sea.

Thy loving eyes with joy will beam,
Your hearts with pleasure beat,
When home again in sweet content
I claim that vacant seat.

Middle East Forces

Just think of the boys of the desert
At war for the sake to be free,
Of the dead, the dying, the injured
And those never again to see.

There's tank, and gun, and aircrews
All sweating and striving to be
'Neath a flag coloured red, white and blue,
Which tells of the land of the free.

What toils and hardships they suffer,
And trying so hard to agree
With the big nobs at home in their comfort,
Responsible for all that's to be.

But soon we hope 'twill be over
And never again to be,
Then those of us still in clover
Return to the land of the free.

Little Wooden Crosses

Little wooden crosses
Bearing name and number,
In the hot dry desert sand
There our comrades slumber.

Lads with whom we laughed and joked
Played games and had our fun,
Lads we slept with 'neath the stars
When the day was done.

Lads we fought beside through hell
Of our race the leaven,
They through tribulation come
Quickly into heaven.

Now beneath the alien earth
Their tired bones rest,
The only epitaph they ask
I tried and gave my best.

But we who live on after them
A great gift too must give
And dedicate our lives to prove
The right to think and live.

The Heart of a Friend

If in the toil of a hard day
You find the hand of a friend
Hold it fast for its gift will last
And keep its faith to the end.

For the hand of a friend is a pledge from the heart
And the heart is the well's spring of love
Love is the truth that makes all things glad
And in it sun shines from the heaven above.

Stand by your friend whatever betide
Your word is what brings him cheer,
If the road seems rough, first a smile is enough,
When it speaks through eyes that are clear.

Let him feel that you know he cannot fail
Though many may pass him by,
The day of living is truly found
If your friend just needs you nigh.

Up the Blue

Up the blue, what memories it brings,
The scorching sun, the blinding dust,
The smell of dead, decaying metal gone to rust,
The drone of planes,
The scream of bombs, a moan or two.
Then silence as we gaze around
With unshed tears on what remains
Comrades gone beyond all aid
Another debt which must be paid,
Tourists praised it, Tommies curse it
As they battle for the future, hoping
That when it is over, comfort in their
Homes they'll find knowing
Well their duties done,
But thinking of the time.

The Man England Forgot

I'm out in the desert, I feel all alone
Patiently waiting a letter from home,
So many have written but none have I had
I feel I'm forgotten, I sometimes feel sad.

They say I belong to the MEFs
For the sake of my country, my home that I left.
But no news have I had, do I matter or not
Or am I the one, the man England forgot?

The mail's just arrived with the stories from the base
With heart beating fast, to the crowd make haste
Eagerly waiting my name to be called,
My hopes dashed to pieces, I hear that is all.

Back to my tent, I slowly tread,
My thoughts all a turmoil, my head like lead.
Am I forgotten do I matter or not,
Or am I the one, the man England forgot?

Some get parcels, letters, cards and cablegrams too,
Some get mail from the friends they know;
Their faces all bright with eager delight,
The pleasure it gives is plain to my sight.

I think of my loved ones, I think of my friends
And wonder just what's happening to them.
Is there a friend who cares just one jot,
Or am I the one, the man England forgot?

The days come and go, they seem like years,
As I think of my home there's often a tear.
Through battles I've been, my duty for you,
How near to death God only knew.

My task would be easy, I'd not care a jot
If one letter I'd had, or one had I got.
But no mail have I had, they don't care a dot.
Or am I the one, the man England forgot?

A POW's Dawn

Each day the darkness lessens,
Each day the warmth draws near,
Each day brings forth the longing
That the hour of release is near.

The fog of winter is lifting
And the hard cruel frosts as well,
The sun's coming back in the heavens
And the sound of victory bells.

We yearn to be back with our own folks,
We pine for a glimpse of the shores,
Of the dearest land we know of
And forget all discomfort and sores.

Forget too the filth of Derna
And hopeless Benghazi as well,
Dismiss from our minds Attamura
And the other camps that were hell.

The future is what we now live for,
The past is a period dead,
The dread of tomorrow forgotten,
Our thoughts will keep forging ahead.

We pray that it won't be long now
That day of days is at hand,
When once more we'll meet our loved ones
In our own sweet native land.

Desert Rats

We are the boys from every division
Who left our homes "Sir", to make a decision,
For Country and Empire was sorely at stake,
We made up our minds, no enemy would take.

We lived in the desert, out among scrub,
But what did it matter, we did get our grub.
We won, and we lost, Sir, and then won again
Though many a man did suffer much pain.

Then 'twas in June, Sir, when all was not well,
Our Officers spoke, but only to tell
The enemy were here, with thousands of men
And that little town we had to defend.

The battle did rage for just a few days
And now all is over, what can we say.
We did what was told, Sir, and not what we thought,
So perhaps that's the reasons we all got caught.

He bunched us together, and drove us along
But no one lost heart, Sir, among that great throng.
We sorted ourselves and each found a mate
And swore to share whatever our fate.

In transport we travelled, packed tight together
For many a mile in hottest of weather,
Until we arrived, Sir, at a barbed-wire pen,
The best they could do, for us thousands of men.

'Twas many weeks later and most of us sick,
We got on a boat, Sir, for another rough trip.
Hungry and tired we crossed the sea,
Only to arrive here, in Italy.

Prisoners of War, Sir, was what we were told,
Here in a land, that for centuries old
Was the home of the Christian, in every land,
But not so in these days for this little band.

Now our day is coming, as we all can see
When this war will end, and we shall be free
And all we've experienced, Sir, hateful and rotten
Forever and all time, will be forgotten.

Fort Mechili

Dark tired shins and hearts like rock,
They stood to meet the German shock.
Rifles in their hands became
Their passport to the hall of fame.

Give in, they did not know the word,
They fought alike with curse and sword,
And died like heroes from a book
With a bold and fearless look.

England has the right to be
Proud of men who fought like these
And gave their lives for liberty.
"Was it worth it?" we shall see.

The Life of a POW

We are but POWs
And lead a funny life,
Away from harm and danger
And free from toil and strife.

We have no occupation
And neither toil nor spin,
No work of any kind to do,
All day to do it in.

We wake up every morning
From our palliasse of straw,
When we hear the cry of ''coffee up''
They bring it through the door.

Then we drink but half a mug
Of liquid dark and warm
That milk and sugar never seen
In any shape or form.

Then down go all our heads again
Until 'tis half-past ten
When the "Grub up,
Come and get it" cry
Awakens all the men.

What is this grub they shout about
So early in the day?
A tiny little bit of cheese
That a mouse could put away.

And a loaf of bread that is
So small and brown and light
That would not tax the strength
Of a healthy three-year-old child to bite.

A little bit of onion
Completes this lovely feast
And to state, that we're still hungry,
Well that's saying the very least.

. . . . . *continued*

Then there's not much else to do
For the rest of all the day,
No books to read, little to smoke,
No games at all to play.

Some sit and talk,
Some sit and think
Or by drawing the time employ,
But we have one common hobby,
Tons of lice to destroy.

We do not fear the machine gun
Or Jerry bomb or shell,
But to the day we're homeward bound
Our thoughts do always dwell.

We sit and listen to griff
And pass the rumours round,
Dream of the day when this life is past
And at Home Sweet Home we're found.

Then the bugle sounds the Roll Call
And they count us one by one,
For the time is passing, now lads
And the day is nearly done.

The only thing now is skilly,
Which we drink in half a minute
And it's lucky if we find
Rice or macaroni in it.

Then finally we finish
With a Red Cross cup of tea
With the consolation that
From over eating we're kept free.

Then after a little chat
Again lay down our weary heads
To pass away another night
Upon our four-man beds.

To dream of home and firesides bright
And good hot meals once more,
Eat all we want without dividing
Each scrap of food by four.

Plenty of wholesome bread and cheese,
Cakes and pastries too,
Biscuits, sweets and chocolate,
Dishes old and new.

But cheer up lads ne'er despair
For the time will come at last
When this life like an evil dream
Is over, done and past.

Then their bits of bread and cheese
And macaroni they can keep,
As with well-filled bellies once more
We on decent beds do sleep.

CARPI PG 73, Spring 1943:

Four fellow POWs:
Bill Lack (?/Armstrong), Cliff Nichols, Jack Smith and Alf Kelsell.

Little Brown Loaf

Ha, Ha, Ha, He, He, He,
Little brown loaf, don't I love thee.
From starvation I'm kept free,
Little brown loaf, because of thee.

I line up every morn,
And view you with dismay,
To think that you are all the bread,
I've got to eat today.

You're sometimes long, sometimes short,
And often squashed out flat
And sometimes have a hole inside
That would hold a baby rat.

And sometimes like a sausage roll
With a mouse bite at the end,
Indeed you are a sorry sight
My little brown skinned friend.

Your weight it is 200 grammes
That's what the Eyeties say
But I think about 100
Must have dropped off on the way.

You are so light, that a small tom cat
Would lift you up with ease.
Shall I put the cheese between you,
Or you between the cheese?

I pick you up and turn you round,
About and upside down,
But you don't grow any larger
Oh, my little loaf of brown.

To the cookhouse I would go
To change thee for another,
But awaiting there for me I fear,
An even smaller brother.

I cut you into slices small
To make you look a lot.
Your size it really doth appal,
But you are all I've got.

And if my wishes could come true
Behind that cookhouse door,
I'd eat you up a dozen times
And then have room for more.

But when I'm back in Blighty boy,
And that's the place for me,
And walking down the local street
A baker's shop I see.
Priced at a penny for two
Some rolls, I'll stop and think again,
Oh little brown loaf, of you,

And wonder how we lived on thee
In that land of want and dread,
Then go inside and buy
A real British loaf of bread.

Neighbourly POWs

Now old Prisoner Binks and old Prisoner Johns
Each shared a Red Cross parcel, about so long,
And the only way it could be divided
Was to cut all in half, and take left or right,
Just which is decided
And all was peaceful and calm as a cow
Till one of the dopes started a row.

Old Prisoner Binks declared with some grit,
That it was his turn to have the odd biscuit,
But old Prisoner Johns said he'd see Binks to Norwich
Before Binks should have that one odd biscuit.
Binks added a dozen to each word of Johns
And soon they were going at it, hammer and tongs
And they each vowed in his heart, that he would not take
That round Service biscuit, till the other said shake.

The day grew so long for old Binks and old Johns
They did not whistle, nor ne'er have a song
And there in that Red Cross box a stranger crept in
And was busy examining the contents of that tin
And I wonder just what old Johns and Binks would think
When they found what had happened, there would be a stink.
Then all of a sudden old Prisoner Binks
Started scratching his head and did a big think,
For a long time he scratched looking worried and grave
When all of a sudden he had a brainwave,
His stomach was aching, it was full of air,
So of that biscuit resolved to have his share.

When the time came for retiring to rest
To deceive Prisoner Johns, Prisoner Binks did his best,
He jumped on his bed and banged on the boards,
Took off his boots, dropped them on the floor
And soon he was making a row like an elephant roaring,
To make Prisoner Johns think he was in bed a-snoring,
And when all was quiet, he peeped out of the clothes,
Then crawled on all fours, in the dark of the night,
Then all of a sudden he had a great fright,
There in front of him, two eyes shining green and bright
And e'er he could call to is partner in bed
Something as hard as a brick hit the top of his head
And without a murmur or so much as a groan,
He dropped flat on his back and lay dead as a stone.

When Binks came to, he was lying in bed
Old Prisoner Johns was bathing his head
And looking at Johns and uttering a curse,
"What hit me?" he said "Pray tell me the worse."
Prisoner Johns did a laugh and touching his brow,
"'Twas my head that hit you, most strange to allow."

Now old Prisoner Binks, and old Prisoner Johns
Again share with each other their parcel so long,
But alas, most sad to relate,
Neither had the biscuit that started this rot,
Mr Mouse had got in and devoured the lot
And all that was left was the plain cardboard box.

Yes, POWs , as you have been taught,
Sometimes in two minds, there's but one single thought
Each that same night had decided to take
His share of the biscuit and leave the other to his mate,
But being so dark and groping about
They bumped their old heads a hell of a clout
The biscuit they lost so much to their sorrow,
So, I leave it to you POWs
To think out the moral.

Just a Thought

Here's to the lads, who are prisoners of war
Especially those from the land we adore,
May this painful existence come to an end
It won't be long now, it's just round the bend.

Let's spare a thought for those not here
For those who'll ne'er again stand to cheer,
They've given their lives for the sake to be free
It might have been you, but it had to be he.

We've a lot to be thankful for those of us here
And a lot to look forward to this coming year,
It's just a thought on ending these lines
Let's join in the chorus of
Auld Lang Syne.

Ode to a POW

You've all seen a lion caged in a show
Who paces around, nowhere to go
A POW feels just the same,
Playing this hopeless silly game.
Instead of steel, it's rows of barbed wire,
Sentries outside, just ready to fire,
So we just plod around, dressed up like a dud,
Up to our eyes in slime and soft mud.

It's lovely here when the rain comes down
Pools of water in which you could drown
So we just get back to our huts and our beds
And try to get some sleep instead.
Now you would think this all rather nice
But you should see the swarms of lice,
They long for that time when you get into bed
And try to rest your weary head.
They all race to see who can bite you first,
Gor blimey, don't you shout and curse.
You take off your shirt and throw it away
And pray that tomorrow will be a fine day.

Then there's the Roll Call, oh what a game
Counting you all, again and again.
Sometimes it's right, sometimes it's wrong,
So you patiently wait, along with the throng.

All this time, your anger does mount,
Then you find there's another recount.
After some hours you go on your way,
Roll Call's over for another day.

Now you ought to see, it fair makes you scream,
A loaf is what it should have been.
It's ever so small, just like a wee roll,
To keep together your body and soul.

. . . . . *continued*

A museum to keep it is the place,
Always on show, on a lovely glass case.
Placed by its side, a sight sure to please,
Your daily ration of issue cheese.

Then there's skilly of macaroni and rice,
To see anything in it, you've got to look twice.
If you ever find "veg", don't throw a fit,
Be fair with your mate and give him a bit.
So, now I'll finish and go on my way,
Sorry to tell you, my sad tale of woe.

Joe's Offensive

'Tis a wintery morning in Russia.
The Jerries are freezing and numb,
Instead of advance, they're retreating,
For the Russian offensive's begun.

Stalingrad, which the Jerries had taken
Is recaptured through ice, snow and mud,
The German "sixth" army is slaughtered,
In a welter of sweat and blood.

Some Rumanian divisions were with them,
They've paid the full price for their pains,
Part of Goering's great *Luftwaffe* is shattered,
Stalingrad one of Russia's great gains.

Rostov and Karkov retaken
By Russians who never tire,
They are chasing the Germans to Poland,
Regardless how heavy the fire.

We take off our hats to the Russians,
Hard fighting their spirits can't bend,
They'll chase Jerry back to his homeland
And bring this damn war to an end.

The Glamorous East

Baksheesh, Sahib, hear the cry
On every hand as we go by
Whining beggars, filthy scum,
Never wash, from sun to sun.
Chicoes dirtier than the dust
Confront us with hands out-thrust,
Glamorous East, the writers write,
Easily said when out of sight.

Shoeshine Sahib, shoeshine boy,
Smites our ears as we deploy.
Camel stench is in the air,
Donkeys braying everywhere.
Flies around us buzz and bite,
Filth to left and filth to right.
Glamorous East the poets say
Easily said when far away.

Cries of London once again,
There's music in that sweet refrain.
Green and lovely countryside,
Peace and happiness there abide.
We'll go there some summer's day,
We'll go there and go to stay.
Glamorous East, the silly fools,
Should have stayed in Sunday School.

Waiting

When you're far away from the one you love
Stop and gaze at the heavens above,
Whether the time be sun-scorched noon
Or a frosty night with a glittering moon.

And there up above in that realm of space,
I see not the sun or moon, but a face,
A beautiful face with a tender smile,
Which tells me she's waiting to make life worthwhile.

Perhaps tonight from her windowpane
She's gazing aloft, on her lips my name,
As she prays to God, way up above,
To watch over, keep safe and return that love.

So when you're feeling alone and forlorn,
Watch into the night, and the wakening morn
And remember that westward across the blue,
She's watching and waiting the same as you.

A Stirrer-up of Skilly

Some talk of the funny jobs, that they have been and got
But I think you will agree, that mine's the strangest of the lot,
The latest one I have found, though to you it may sound silly,
I'm a skilly stirrer-upper. Yes a stirrer-up of skilly.

It is a most important job, inside a prison camp
And as a skilly stirrer, I really am a champ.
Although the hours are not so long and the pay is nowt,
I have to be quite skilful and know what I'm about.

I take my stand inside the hut, just up against the wall
And wait there fit and ready, when I hear the "scoff-up" call
I hold a piece of wood, that is just like a stick
And grasp it firmly in the hand, when I hear the door latch click.

They bring the skilly right inside, the interest is immense
And the boys stand round awaiting for the stirrer to commence.
The dixies small, are all lined up on't floor in bright array,
For this is surely one of the most important times of day.

The corporals, two, are standing there, with tin mugs at the slope,
For we shall have some skilly now, at least that's what we hope.
The carriers take the lid off and a cloud of steam does rise,
It smells just like a London fog, and brings tears to the eyes.

Some say it's thick, some say it's thin and others NBG,
But like muddy water on the Thames, it always seems to me.
Then I digs my stick in and sweeps it round and round
Being very careful not to spill any on the ground.

The corporals then with mugs in hand immediately start fishing,
The lads look on with eager eyes, for a good catch fondly wishing.
Ah, one has caught a piece of turnip right at the commence,
Another a piece of carrot spies, excitement is intense.

The piece of macaroni tries to glide away in vain
But with uncanny skill, he's caught and trapped again.
An inch of cabbage slips away, a piece of spud is seen
And when the latter's seen, oh what competition keen.

All the time I keeps astirring round and round
Until at last the tide goes down, and dixie bottom found
One day when't lid was lifted, as I stood there with my stick
I could not shove it in the stuff, it was so blooming thick.

The cause of this strange accident investigation proved
That the cooks own private dixie from its usual place had moved
And got mixed up with others standing there upon the floor,
Which made these poor chaps tear their hair and stamp and roar.

And since that day to prevent such a terrible thing occurring again,
They fixed it firmly to the wall with padlock strong and chain,
But soon now I shall get the sack and be on the dole once more,
For they tell me that it won't be long till again we're on England's shore.

And shortly we shall see again, the good old Cliffs of Dover
And none of us will want that skilly, when once this war is over
And in years to come when my small boy will read his history book,
He'll turn to me one night and say with quite a knowing look
"What did you do in the war, Dad, and what part did you play?"
A couple of buttons will pop off, as I turn to him and say,
"Why, I won the war in Carpi, don't you know, silly-billy,
For I was the champion stirrer. Yes a stirrer-up of skilly."

POSTSCRIPT

"My father was a patriot through and through. His love and pride of his country never wavered to the day he died and never regretted volunteering for service. I wish he could have seen this book of his in print, he would have been very proud. These closing words he often repeated in his later years . . . . 'There'll always be an England'." (The author's daughter Janet)

The author was born in Stannington, Sheffield, but lived most of his life in Rossington, and Cantley near Doncaster.